2/16

ARCTIC WHITE

ARCTIC WHITE

Danna Smith

Illustrated by **Lee White**

HENRY HOLT AND COMPANY • NEW YORK

Henry Holt and Company, LLC
Publishers since 1866
175 Fifth Avenue, New York, New York 10010
mackids.com

Library of Congress Cataloging-in-Publication Data
Smith, Danna.
Arctic white / Danna Smith ; illustrated by Lee White.
pages   cm
Summary: "A young girl looks around her home in the arctic and sees only white, white, white.
But one day her grandfather takes her out on a journey across the tundra. And at the end of their
cold walk, the dark opens up to show the Northern Lights dancing across the sky—blue, green,
and purple"—Provided by publisher.
ISBN 978-1-62779-104-5 (hardback)
[1. Winter—Fiction. 2. Auroras—Fiction. 3. Grandfathers—Fiction. 4. Arctic regions—Fiction.]
I. White, Lee, 1970– illustrator. II. Title.
PZ7.S644649Ar 2016   [E]—dc23   2015003250

Henry Holt books may be purchased for business or promotional use. For information on bulk purchases,
please contact the Macmillan Corporate and Premium Sales Department at (800) 221-7945 x5442 or
by e-mail at specialmarkets@macmillan.com.

First Edition—2016 / Book design by Véronique Lefèvre Sweet
The illustrations in this book were created using watercolor and ink on Arches cold-pressed paper,
then digitally enhanced.
Printed in China by RR Donnelley Asia Printing Solutions Ltd., Dongguan City, Guangdong Province

10 9 8 7 6 5 4 3 2 1

For Boston and Olivia
—D. S.

For Emerson
—L.W.

When you live in the Arctic in winter,
everything is a shade of white.

The blue-white of the tundra.
The yellow-white of the polar bear.
The silver-white of the arctic fox.

Sometimes, when you wish on a star for more color,
you get only gray.
And gray is still a shade of white.

Here, winter days are dark as night.
As time passes, you wonder:
Where did all the color go?
Did the wind blow it away?

Every day you hope for more color.
Grandfather says hope is golden.
You can only see it when you
look into a snowy owl's eyes.

Every day you wait for more color.
You wait and wait in the white.

Then one night you hear a hum in the air.
Your grandfather smiles.
You think he might be keeping a secret.

You bundle up and
follow him outside.

When you live in the Arctic, the cold always finds
a way to sneak inside your warmest parka.

Your grandfather's lantern glows bright.
Together, you go on a journey,
gathering friends along the way—
friends who hope for color, too.

You trudge across the tundra,
past the icy sea and sleeping seals.
Even footprints are white in the Arctic.

You climb a snowy mountain and find a good spot,
a place your grandfather says is close to the secret.
There you sit and wait.

Tonight you welcome the darkness
because you need dark to see . . .

the Northern Lights.

Purple swirling.
Green glowing.
Blue swooping.
Red pulsing—like your heartbeat.

You watch colors dance across the sky,
and you forget all about the cold.

The colors lighten the night,
bright enough to see the lines
on your grandfather's face
and the twinkle in his eye.

Too soon, the colors begin to fade.
You keep watching until the sky
is as dark as before.

You make your way down the snowy mountain,
past the icy sea and sleeping seals.

Back home, you remember the colors.

Purple swirling.
Green glowing.
Blue swooping.
Red pulsing.

When you live in the Arctic in winter,
everything is a shade of white.
But inside, there is hope.